W9-BDC-797

By JANICE DEAN "The Weather Machine"

Illustrated by RUSS COX

Library of Congress Control Number: 2014945283
ISBN 978-1-62157-254-1

Published in the United States by
Regnery Kids
An imprint of Regnery Publishing
A Salem Communications Company
300 New Jersey Avenue NW
Washington, DC 20001
www.RegneryKids.com

Manufactured in the United States of America
10 9 8 7 6 5 4 3 2 1

Distributed to the trade by
Perseus Distribution
250 West 57th Street
New York, NY 10107

To Matthew and Theodore. Like little snowflakes, you are special, unique, and so precious.

Field trip!

Freddy's class was visiting the Frog News Network, and he couldn't wait to show his friends around.

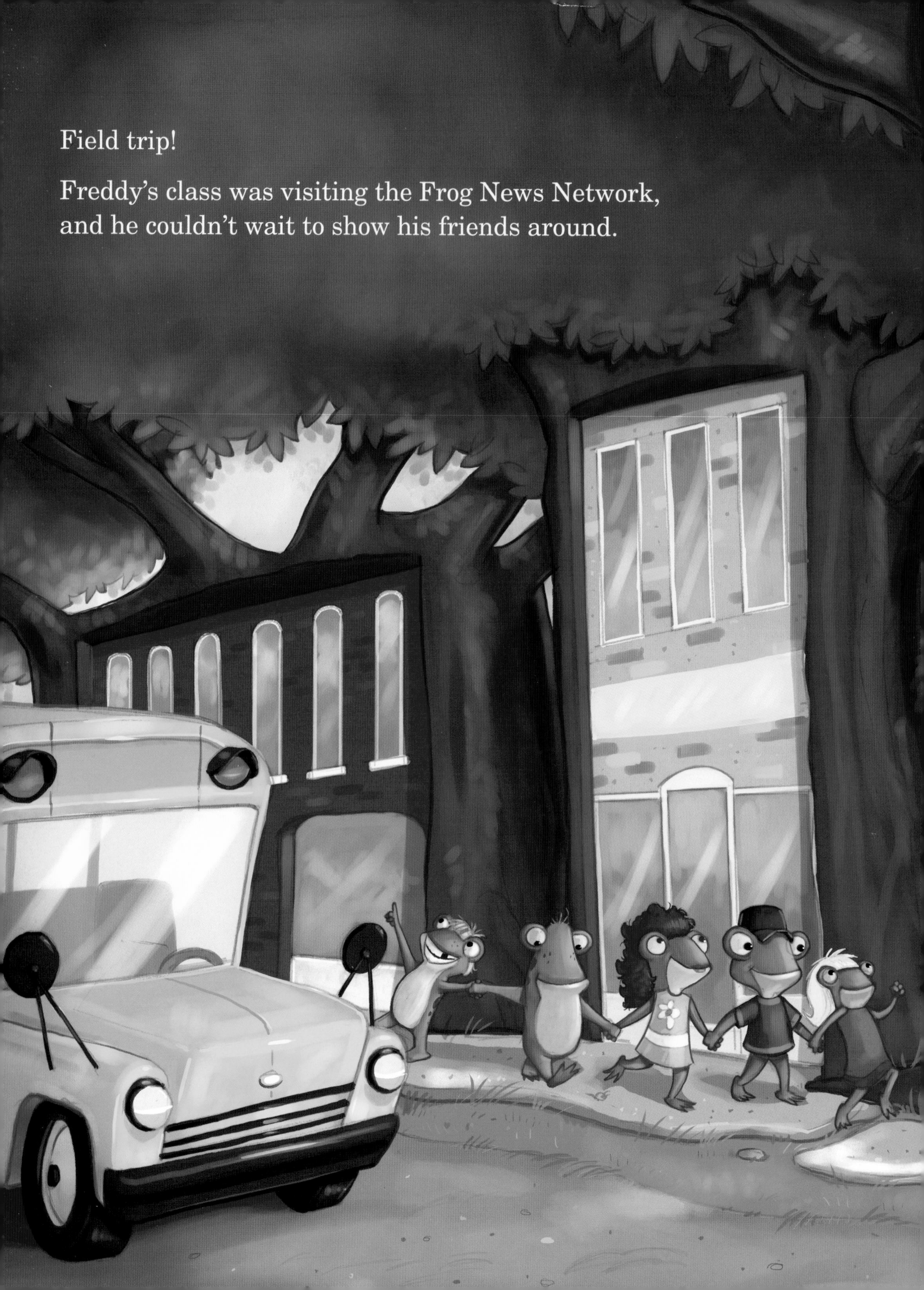

Freddy was known all around town as a weather expert. He had his own backyard weather station. He had a special job working at the Frog News Network, too.

Whenever Sally Croaker and Polly Woggins needed an extra set of webbed hands, they called on Freddy. He was always happy to hop in to help out after school.

“Hey, look at me,” said Gill Flipper. “I’m a frogcaster too.”

Everyone looked at the television monitor and started to laugh. Gill was pretending to do the weather in front of the big green screen. But his classmates only saw two eyeballs and a big mouth. Where was he?

"Hey, what's so funny?" demanded Gill. Freddy clicked a button, and the green screen turned blue. Presto! Gill was back.

Now Gill was laughing too. "It's not easy being green!"

Freddy pointed to an image on his computer screen. “This just came in from our weather satellite. See the big comma shape? That’s a winter storm we’re watching.

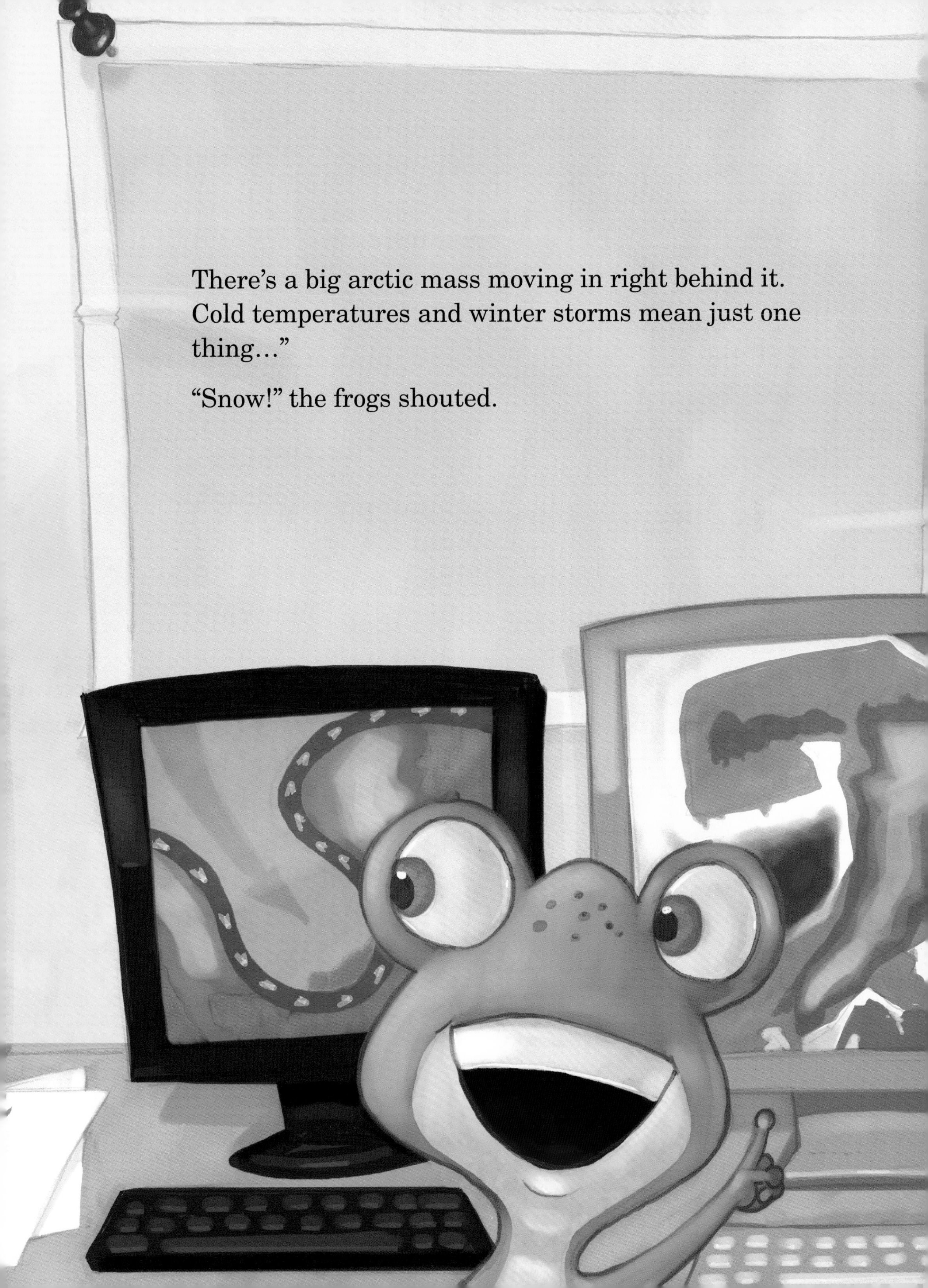

There's a big arctic mass moving in right behind it. Cold temperatures and winter storms mean just one thing…"

"Snow!" the frogs shouted.

Freddy wasn't quite as excited as his classmates. This storm was packing more than a few fluffy snowflakes. The whole town could get snowed in! Freddy had to do something BEFORE the big blizzard hit.

There was just one problem…

All his friends wanted to talk about was building snow frogs, snowball fights, and a day off from school!

"What do we have here?" a deep voice croaked from the doorway. It was the mayor with Sally Croaker and Polly Woggins. How exciting to see three of Lilypad's most famous celebrities!

"Sally and Polly tell me that there's a big blizzard heading toward Lilypad," said the mayor. "What do you think, Freddy?"

MAYOR

MAYOR

Freddy checked his maps again. Snow. Cold temperatures. Wind. Hmm…

"Yes, Mr. Mayor," Freddy said. "All the weather clues point to a big blizzard blowing in tonight."

"Sounds like we have some work to do," the mayor exclaimed. "Like my good friend Freddy always says…"

"Be prepared!" exclaimed Sally and Polly.

Be prepared! This advice worked last summer when a big thunderstorm threatened to soak the town's annual picnic. Being prepared on that day meant umbrellas and moving indoors.

But this was different…How do you prepare for a big blizzard with snow and ice and—brrr—freezing temperatures?

There wasn't a minute to spare, so Freddy got to work. He made a list of all the things frogs needed to stay safe and warm during a blizzard.

Freddy printed copies of his blizzard list to show Sally and Polly. When he found Polly, she was too excited to look. "I get to do live reports from the news van right in the middle of the storm," she said. "Wow!"

Freddy wasn't sure this was a good idea. "Polly, blizzards are dangerous!"

"Oh Freddy, don't be a worrywart. I'll be fine." Polly patted his head. Then she set off to look for purple mittens to match her purple hat.

When he got home, Freddy dashed through the house gathering supplies for not one, but two, weather emergency kits. He found two red bags and labeled one “Freddy’s Big Blizzard Kit” and the other “Polly’s Big Blizzard Kit.”

“Mom, I need to take this to Polly before the storm gets bad.” The winds were already picking up, and the temperature was dropping fast.

Freddy found Polly with her crew loading the news van with camera gear. He told her about the blizzard kit and encouraged her to take it with her. "Oh, Freddy, don't you worry about me," Polly said sweetly. "I know what I'm doing."

But Freddy was worried. He tucked Polly's blizzard kit in the van—just in case.

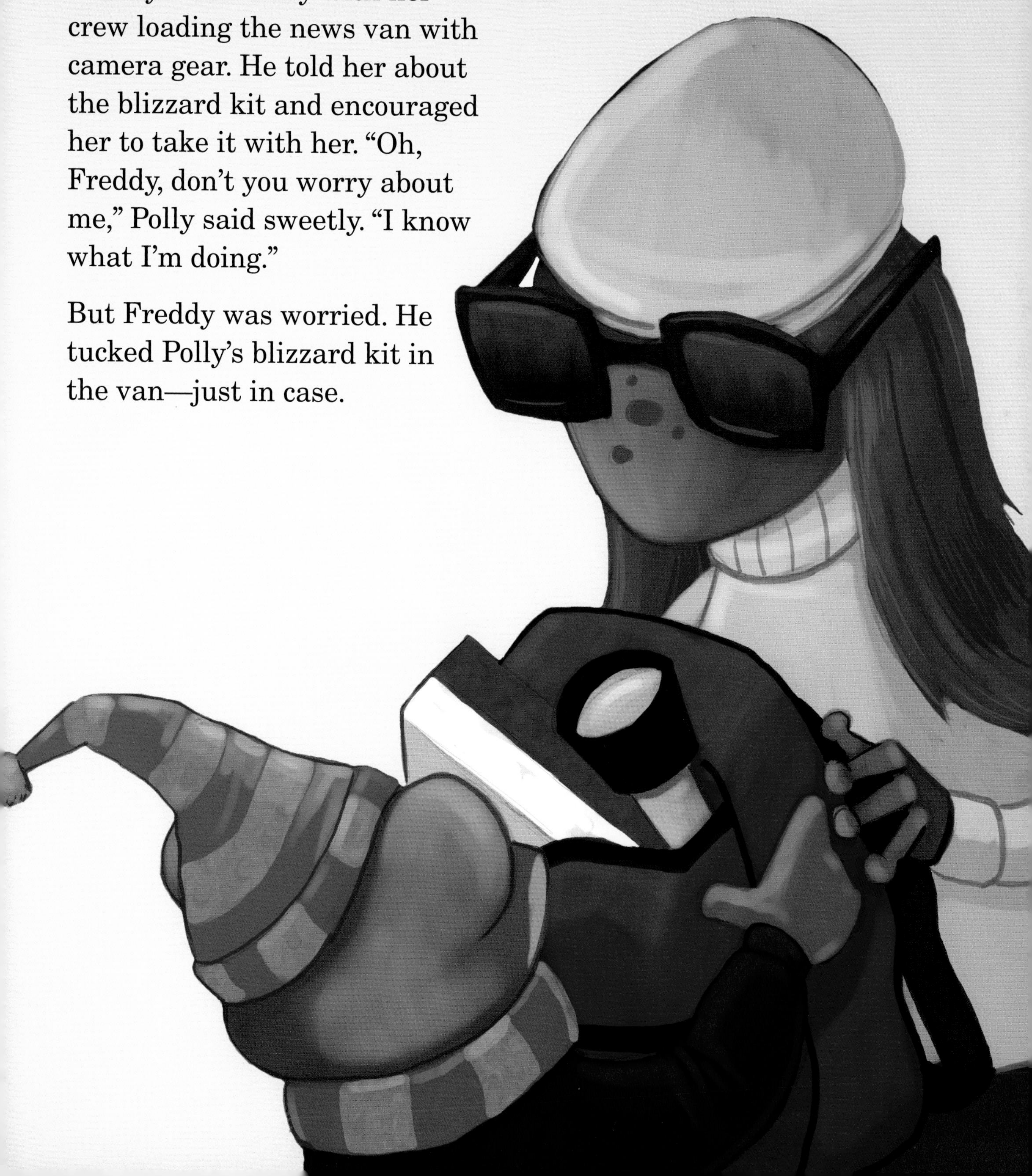

When Freddy got home, his mom had a bowl of fried cricket stew ready for him. He ate in the living room and watched Sally Croaker's forecast.

"And now let's go to Polly Woggins on the scene with an update." The camera view went to Polly. She was shivering outside on a snowy street corner.

"This blizzard is moving in fast with heavy snow and howling winds. And, believe me, folks, it is really cold out here! This is Polly Woggins reporting live from the corner of..."

Just then, the television screen went completely black, and so did all the lights in Freddy's house!

The electricity was out! That meant no TV, no lights, and no heat.

Thanks to Freddy's blizzard kit, they had plenty of bottled water and canned food.

Freddy got his flashlight and weather radio out to listen for the latest storm reports. They would be safe and warm inside while the blizzard raged outside.

But what about Polly? Was she okay?

The next morning, Freddy hopped out of bed to look out the window. Wow! Freddy had never seen so much snow in his life!

The lights were back on. Freddy hurried to the living room to turn on the TV. “This blizzard is one for the record books,” Sally reported. “Lilypad has never had this much snow.”

Sally looked tired, but she was okay. But where was Polly?

Just then, the camera went to an outdoor view. Whew! Polly was safe. "The news van got stuck in the snow, and they just dug us out," Polly explained. "Thanks to Freddy leaving this blizzard kit, we were prepared."

Sally looked into the camera, smiled, and said, “Friends, you heard it here first. Freddy the Frogcaster has saved the day once again!”

By noon, snowplows had cleared the streets and frogs were venturing outside. After all his hard work, Freddy was ready for some fun.

He met up with his friends at the park. Everyone was bundled up and enjoying the snow. Some were building snow frogs. Others were packing snowballs.

Gill Flipper waved to Freddy from the top of Toad Hill. Freddy grabbed his sled and hurried up to join him, happily shouting, "SNOW DAY!"

Hi, Friends!

Brrrr…

It's cold outside! It's winter time here in Lilypad, and we are still digging out from the big blizzard you just read about. I learned so much about winter storms, and I can't wait to share it with you!

One of the best things I learned is that winter storms usually give plenty of clues. These clues give weather forecasters (and frogcasters!) time to warn people to be prepared.

A cold **AIR MASS** is the first clue we look for. An air mass is a big area of weather that has the same composition. Two types of air masses must come together for a winter storm to form. One air mass must be very cold, and the other warm and moist. Where these two types of air masses come together we call a **FRONT**. This is like a divider or line that separates one air mass from another. If the cold air pushes the warm air out of the way, this will be called a cold front. When warm air moves in and rides up and over the heavier cold air mass, it is called a warm front. If neither of these air masses moves, it is called a stalled or stationary front.

Air Mass

The next weather clue is **WATER VAPOR**. Water vapor is water in the form of a gas instead of liquid (like rain in a puddle) or solid (like an ice cube). You may not always see water vapor, but it's all around us and helps make snow and clouds. Some winter days are so cold you can see your breath. The

cloudy fog you see when you breathe out of your mouth is water vapor. Cool, right?

When temperatures drop low enough, water vapor condenses and freezes into little patterns of ice crystals. The ice crystals attach themselves to little bits of dirt or dust in the atmosphere. These crystals get stuck together and—ta-da!—snowflakes are formed.

Did you know each snowflake is six-sided and made of as many as two hundred ice crystals? As the snow crystals grow, they become heavier and fall from the clouds.

By the way, did you know that no two snowflakes are alike? It's true. A scientist named Wilson Bentley ("The Snowflake Man") proved it back in the early 1900s. He found a way to catch snowflakes and keep them cold enough to take a picture. He had pictures of more than a thousand snowflakes and discovered they were all unique. Just like you and me!

Snow isn't the only type of winter precipitation. **FROST** is another type. Frost is ice crystals that form on surfaces like a rooftop or the grass or the leaves of plants when the temperature drops below freezing and the water vapor (the invisible gas we can't usually see) freezes into ice crystals. We usually see frost in the morning before the sun melts it away. Frost is more of a problem for plants than it is for people. That's why farmers stay on the lookout for "Jack Frost's visits" in the weeks between seasons. They have to be prepared to protect their crops from freezing.

SLEET is another type of winter precipitation. Sleet is raindrops that freeze into ice pellets before they hit the ground. Sleet usually bounces when hitting a surface and does not stick to objects. Sleet can accumulate like snow and can be a nuisance to cars, people, and frogs who are outside during a sleet storm.

FREEZING RAIN is another, more dangerous, type of winter precipitation. It is a liquid (rain) that falls into a shallow layer of freezing air. It then forms a coating of ice on bridges, roads, power lines, and trees. It causes cars, people, and even frogs to slip and slide all over the place. My advice for staying safe during a freezing-rain storm is to stay inside until it melts!

Of course, my favorite type of winter precipitation is snow, snow, and more snow! And that brings me back to **BLIZZARDS**. A blizzard is a long-lasting winter storm with strong winds, blowing snow, and dangerous wind chills. Sometimes strong winds pick up snow that's already fallen and create something called a "ground blizzard."

The National Weather Service defines a blizzard as a storm that contains a large amount of snow or blowing snow with winds over thirty-five miles per hour and visibilities of less than a quarter of a mile for at least three hours.

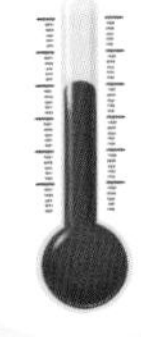

Traveling in a blizzard can become dangerous or even impossible because of the strong winds and blowing snow. When the wind and snow are especially strong, it creates "whiteout conditions." When this happens, travelers have no choice but to pull off the road because it is impossible to see where they are going.

WIND CHILL results when strong winds and cold temperatures combine. Wind chill makes it "feel" even colder than it is. My favorite thing to do when there is wind chill is to stay inside in front of a toasty fire and drink hot cocoa. When people have to go outside in these conditions, it is important to have every inch of skin covered by super-warm hats, gloves, coats, and boots. And not just because your mom or dad says so. Frostbite (damage to skin that's exposed to freezing temperatures) or hypothermia (a dangerous drop in body temperature) can cause big—even life-threatening—problems. Yikes!

Here is a fun little riddle for you: What is it called when snow comes with lightning and thunder?

THUNDERSNOW! This doesn't happen often, but when it does—wow! Thundersnow is very similar to summertime thunderstorms—an intense storm with thunder and lightning. The one difference is that thundersnow storms tend to be quieter since the snow muffles the sound of thunder.

Our blizzard in Lilypad brought a record-breaking amount of snow. One day back in 1921, a place called Silver Lake in Colorado got seventy-six inches. That's over six feet of snow in one day! Can you even imagine? I'm really glad our Lilypad didn't get that much!

Mountains get a lot more snow than flat places. There is a mountain called Mount Rainier in Washington where it snows every month of every year. One year there was a total of 1,224 inches of snow. Good thing all that snow didn't come at once!

Now, my weather-loving friends, you know as much as I do about winter weather. But, if you are like me, you'll want to learn more. I'll keep digging for information and will share it online at my website at www.RegneryKids.com. Most of all, remember the number one rule about staying safe in winter weather is to **BE PREPARED**!

Your weather-loving friend,

Freddy

P.S. About that green screen in the story...the green screen didn't work out so well for my friend Gill. He is a green frog after all. But green screens work just fine for meteorologists like my friend Janice Dean "The Weather Machine." She uses a green screen (chroma key is its real name) to do weather forecasts every single day. So even though it looks like she's pointing to weather maps, she's really pointing to a blank green screen. A computer program puts maps (or any object) into a video screen that shows up on your television screen.

Winter Storm Checklist

How can you be prepared for winter weather emergencies? This is how I do it. First, I think about the problems that can come with bad weather. You know, all the "what if" questions. Then I think of ways to be prepared for those "what ifs." That's when I pull out my red backpack and fill it up with the supplies my family needs to stay safe and warm when bad weather comes our way.

You can do this too. Here are some winter "what if" questions along with ideas for solving them. Ask your family to help you be prepared!

WHAT IF…temperatures drop and the weather gets really cold?

- ❑ Blankets
- ❑ Extra warm clothing
  (sweaters, hats, scarves, coats, gloves, mittens, and boots)

WHAT IF…all the lights go out?

- ❑ Flashlights
- ❑ Extra batteries

WHAT IF…the power goes out and we can't watch news updates on television?

- ❑ Hand-crank, solar-powered, or battery-operated radio
- ❑ Solar-powered phone chargers

WHAT IF…we get snowed in and can't go to the store for food?

- ❑ Bottled water
- ❑ Juice pouches
- ❑ Ready-to-eat canned foods
- ❑ Can opener
- ❑ Non-perishable pasteurized milk
- ❑ Cereal
- ❑ Protein bars

- ❑ Fruit snacks
- ❑ Nuts and nut butters
- ❑ Favorite treats
- ❑ Pre-packaged baby food
- ❑ Pet food

WHAT IF…someone gets hurt or ill during the storm?

- ❑ First aid kit (stocked with bandages, antibacterial ointment, hydrocortisone, thermometer, and other basic medical supplies and medicines)
- ❑ Always call 911 in an emergency

WHAT IF…we get bored waiting for the snow to melt?

- ❑ Puzzles
- ❑ Games
- ❑ Activity books

JUST IN CASE we get scared or worried…

Be sure to pack a favorite stuffed animal or blanket to keep you company and help calm the jitters.

REMEMBER your number one job during a winter storm is to stay safe, so...

- Dress warmly
- Eat regularly to give yourself energy
- Drink lots of water
- Keep dry and always change out of wet clothes

WHEN TRAVELING during a winter storm (try really hard not to do this if at all possible!)…

- Take a cell phone and charger
- Keep the gas tank full
- Let friends or neighbors know where you are going
- Keep a winter weather emergency kit in your car
- If you get stuck, stay in your car and wrap up in blankets to stay warm

Acknowledgments

To Roger Ailes, thank you for welcoming me into the Fox Family over a decade ago. Freddy would never have been possible without your support and encouragement.

To Dianne Brandi, for always keeping your door open for me. I am thankful for your advice, kindness, and honesty.

To Peter and Cheryl Barnes for their “leap of faith” on my children’s book idea.

To Russ Cox. I am in awe of your talent. Thank you for bringing Freddy to life with your brilliant paintbrush.

To all the wonderful people at Regnery Kids for helping my dream of Freddy come true: Marji Ross, Mark Bloomfield, Patricia Jackson, Jason Sunde, and Emily Bruce.

To my editor Diane Reeves, who keeps the frogspeak fresh and exciting while meeting all our deadlines.

To Brandon Noriega, for also being one of my editors—while ensuring my frogcasting/meteorological accuracy is consistent.

To Grandma Stella, Uncle Craig, and Aunt Liz for teaching my boys what family is all about.

To Judy Bristol, for listening and nurturing.

To the thousands of children, parents, grandparents, and teachers who have read Freddy. And to all my fellow meteorologists who used my book to help kids learn about weather in classrooms across the country. I am touched by your support.

And to my husband, Sean. I became the luckiest girl in the world when I met you.

Enjoy more of Freddy's weather adventures in

ISBN: 978-1-62157-084-4

Coming Soon!

Freddy the Frogcaster and the Huge Hurricane!